Samba

in Switzerland

By Paul Yanuziello

Illustrations by Joshua Miller

Samba in Switzerland
Written by Paul Yanuziello
Illustrations by Joshua Miller

First Edition 2022
ISBN Electronic Book: 978-1-7775708-8-0
ISBN Paperback Book: 978-1-7387486-0-0
ISBN Hardcover Book: 978-1-7775708-9-7

Yanuziello, Paul
Samba in Switzerland

Illustrations by Joshua Miller
Cover design by Joshua Miller
Book design by PNJ Services
Copy editor and proofreader: Jennifer D. Foster, Planet Word, lifeonplanetword.wordpress.com

Printed in Canada and the United States of America

Published by PNJ Services

For all of my family, past and present, close and distant, who are always in my thoughts, heart and soul. With all my gratitude and love to the real Samba, an inspiration who will live on through these stories.
~Paul Yanuziello

I dedicate this book to all of my family and friends. Thanks for your support and the great memories that we shared.
~Joshua Miller

A drop of water splashed on Samba's head. He looked up and braced himself for the next wave.

Oh wait, he thought.

His dream of surfing the waves in the city of Rio de Janeiro in Brazil were shattered.

Samba looked around the room, squinting from the early evening sunshine that was in his eyes.
The crystal-clear walls glittered brightly with fairy-tale creatures, then Samba closed his eyes and remembered everything.
He was in the Ice Hotel in Switzerland.

Ariela searched the room. Samba was sound asleep. His legs moved to a shuffle rhythm: *cha-cha, cha, cha-cha, cha-cha, cha.*

It looks like Samba is dancing the samba in his sleep, Ariela thought. Samba slept and danced on. Ariela laughed.

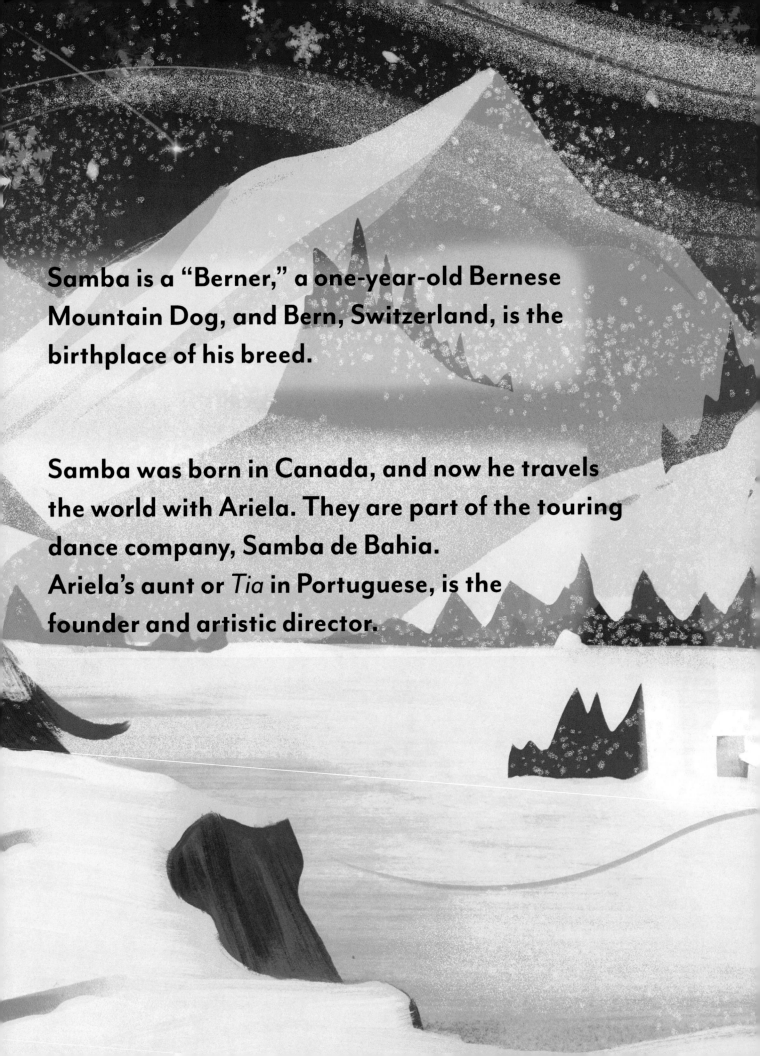

Samba is a "Berner," a one-year-old Bernese Mountain Dog, and Bern, Switzerland, is the birthplace of his breed.

Samba was born in Canada, and now he travels the world with Ariela. They are part of the touring dance company, Samba de Bahia.
Ariela's aunt or *Tia* in Portuguese, is the founder and artistic director.

Thank you, Tia, for this wonderful treat.
One night in the Ice Hotel is magical!
thought Ariela.

Ariela is a ten-year-old Canadian girl. She is
originally from Rio de Janeiro. Her family
brought her to Canada when she was
just a baby.

Samba rolled over and started sliding down the mountain just outside the Ice Hotel. He was moving his legs as fast as he could, but he could not get any traction on the slippery ice.

Suddenly, a strange-looking creature reached out a furry arm and grabbed Samba.

Samba was too thankful to be scared of this weird creature.
"Thanks!" Samba barked.

The creature said, "Don't worry. Just be happy. I don't speak dog, so what are you saying?"
And with that, the creature transformed Samba's barks into words he could understand.

"Who are you? What are you? Some strange type of Swiss dog?" Samba asked the creature. "Hey, what happened to my voice?"

The creature roared with laughter.
"I have been called a dog, but I am not so lucky.
My name is Bertie Barbegazi. I am of the family
Barbegazi, guardians of the treasure of the Alps."

"Treasure?" asked Samba. "Like cookies and pizza?"
Samba sat on Bertie's feet as they skied down the steep
and snowy Swiss mountain.

Bertie explained: "The treasure, Samba, is the beauty of the Alps. That's the treasure I must protect. And I rescue mountain climbers and skiers on occasion. Some people just don't get it."

Finally, Bertie and Samba arrived in Bern. As they entered the town, something knocked Bertie off his feet. Swiss treasure hunters had laid out a trap for him.

Samba went flying through the
air. He was shocked, but not hurt.

"Bertie, are you OK? Can you talk? What should I do?" shouted Samba.
"Go get help, Samba. That's what you can do, and do come back quickly. I am starting to get hungry," Bertie calmly replied.

Samba rushed off toward his family home to get help.

Samba's family had just settled down for dinner. Samba told them all about the Barbegazi he had met.

"Come on! We have to help my friend," barked Samba.
Grandpa Berner said, "Yes, we'll help. But, Samba, do you
want to eat first?"
"Oh yes, of course. What was I thinking? Thanks," Samba
said. "Just a quick bite, then we rescue Bertie."

When the Berners got to the town, Bertie was nowhere to be found. The family of Berners looked accusingly at Samba. Samba said, "Well, Bertie was here. The treasure hunters must have taken him."

The hunters had not gone too far. The Barbegazi had called on the snow with his magic, and he had created an avalanche. The treasure hunters were trapped in the snow.

The Berners also heard the thundering rumble of the snow and headed off in the direction of the avalanche. When they arrived, the Barbegazi was not there.

Samba and his family of Berners dug frantically, and soon the treasure hunters were free. The Berners made them promise to give up treasure hunting and let the Barbegazi be.

If not, the treasure hunters would stay where they were.

The treasure hunters agreed to give up, and they were set free. Bertie Barbegazi made a magical appearance. He seemed happy to see them go.

"Samba, I want to thank you and your family for your help and your bravery. Please accept this gift," said Bertie.
"Thank you, Bertie. You shouldn't have, but I think it's great, just great. What is it?"
"Ah, this is a magical cookie-maker. You can make your own Berner cookies whenever you want," Bertie replied.

"Samba, Samba. *Quer comer!*" Ariela was shaking Samba's shoulder and telling him it was time to eat.

Samba heard Ariela. *Was she trapped in the snow? Oh no!* he thought.

Samba shook his head, licked Ariela's face and then got up excitedly.

He had one quick look around the Ice Hotel, then thought, *No cookie-maker — darn!*

"Where's my cookie-maker?" Samba barked.

And then he dove headfirst into his breakfast.

Ariela laughed. "Were you dreaming, Samba? It sure gave you an appetite. Samba, today we are going to meet your Berner family. So exciting!"

❄ Some Fun Facts for Kids About Switzerland ❄

Switzerland, as of 2021, has a population of 8.6 million people. The capital city of Switzerland is Bern, and it has a population of half a million people. The official name of the country is Swiss Confederation, from *"Confoederatio Helvetica"* in Latin, which means "Swiss Confederation." And that is why the country (telephone dialing) code abbreviation is CH.

Switzerland is a federal republic with 26 cantons, like states or provinces. The coolest canton is the 11th, the canton of Solothurn, where they seem to be obsessed with the number 11. Solothurn is home to 11 museums, 11 fountains, 11 chapels, 11 churches and a town square clock, where the dial only shows 11 hours, not 12.

The languages spoken in Switzerland are varied and include German, French, Italian and Romansh. Romansh is a Romance language indigenous to Switzerland's largest canton, Graubünden, located in the southeastern corner of the country.

Switzerland has the highest mountains in Europe. Forty-eight of the mountains are each more than 13,123 feet (4,000 meters) high. The most famous Swiss mountain is the Matterhorn. The Matterhorn is 14,692 feet (4,478 meters) high and is located near the village of Zermatt. The Toblerone chocolate bar's logo is an image of the Matterhorn.

Each city or region of Switzerland has its own specialty food. For example, flour soup in Basel (*Basler Mehlsuppe*), cherry cake in Zug (*Zuger Kirschtorte*), spiced sausage in Neuenburg/Neuchâtel (*Neuenburger sausage*) and honey cake in Bern (*Berner Honiglebkuchen*).

Switzerland has the best skiing and snowboarding in the world. The country has produced some great athletes, especially in alpine sports. Jan Scherrer, Tanja Frieden and Lara Gut-Behrami are just a few of the Swiss Olympians.

Swiss folklore: The Barbegazi are creatures said to live in the Swiss Alps. According to Swiss and French mythology, they are furry creatures who have big, flat feet and long white beards. Their fur is said to look like icicles. What makes this creature so unique is its kind, well-meaning, helpful nature.

Samba on a Snowy Day

A fun story about a lovable puppy and his best friend on their first snowy adventure. Delight in the magical beauty of a winter wonderland. Enjoy a fast-paced story with thrills and spills — forest trails and mountainous hills — that only a Bernese Mountain Dog like Samba could climb.

What people are saying about *Samba on a Snowy Day*: "This is the perfect read for children thinking of or already owning a larger dog. I found it to be a delightful adventure for younger readers ages 3-6." ~ Alyssa Elmore for Readers' Favorite Book Reviews and Award Contest.

Samba in Brazil

A fun story about a lovable puppy and his best friend on their first overseas vacation. In book 2 of the series, Samba the Bernese Mountain Dog and his best friend are ready for adventure in the land of beautiful beaches, samba dancing and *Carnaval* parades. Cuddle up and join in the merriment with a delightful story that will transport you to a land of incredible beauty. Joshua Miller has captured the majesty of Salvador, Bahia, with breathtaking illustrations.

"...an adorable and fun read. It is informative to the young reader and also introduces them to Portuguese phrases and words. I also liked how the story teaches children about Bernese Mountain dogs and how they aren't exactly equipped for the hot weather of Brazil. The pictures are beautifully done and fit perfectly with the storyline. I can't wait to see what other adventures Ariela and Samba will have." ~ Tiffany Ferrell for Readers' Favorite Book Reviews and Award Contest

Paul Yanuziello is a writer, storyteller, musician, martial arts instructor and an author. The opportunity to write and teach full time in 2017, as well as his passion for teaching and learning from children, became the motivational force to publish his first children's book. In 2019, he published *Samba on a Snowy Day*, to glowing reviews. When Paul is not teaching or learning martial arts, he can be found writing, reading or practising *shinrin-yoku* (forest bathing) in his sanctuary near the Blue Mountains, Ontario, Canada. To keep up to date with Paul, visit paulyanuziello.com and remember to subscribe to his blog, *My Monthly Journal.*

Other books written by Paul Yanuziello with illustrations by Joshua Miller:

Samba in Brazil

Scratchy the Squirrel: A Time for Friends

Joshua Miller is an illustrator, urban sketcher, art instructor and drawing mentor, based in Toronto, Canada. He graduated from the animation program at Seneca College in 2016. Joshua is actively working on his own projects and enjoys experimenting with different illustration styles and approaches. He lends his talents, enthusiasm and energy to learners at the Animation Portfolio Workshop and University of Toronto's School of Continuing Studies, where he was awarded Honorable Mention as one of the top ten instructors. When Joshua is not drawing, he spends his time riding his bike all around the Greater Toronto Area.

Manufactured by Amazon.ca
Bolton, ON

33299210R00026